This book belongs to

To Jay & Ben,
All aboard the Daddy Train

With love
M. M.

This edition published by Parragon Books Ltd in 2014 and distributed by

Parragon Inc.
440 Park Avenue South, 13th Floor
New York, NY 10016

www.parragon.com

Published by arrangement with Gullane Children's Books

Text and illustrations © Mark Marshall 2013

ISBN 978-1-4723-4603-2

Printed in China

The Sleepy Train

Mark Marshall

PaRragon

Bath • New York • Cologne • Melbourne • Delhi
Hong Kong • Shenzhen • Singapore • Amsterdam

Sleepy Train

In pajamas, at the station,
Waiting for a special train.
Chuff-chuff, choo-choo,
Smoke and steam,
Climb aboard and curl up warm!

TICKETS

Driver's engine, clean and smart.
Whistle blows, it's time to start.
Wheels are turning,
Lights aglow,

"All aboard, and off we go!"

Trees speed by,
Getting colder,
Wonder where we're stopping next ...

Penguin shivers. Deep white snow.

"All aboard, and off we go!"

Polar
Station

Jungle rustling, clear night sky,
silver moon is shining bright.
In jumps Monkey, say hello.
"All aboard, and off we go!"

Clickety-clack,
Sleepy Train rumbles.
Dreamy clouds look just like sheep.
Another station. Someone's waiting.

"All aboard, and off we go!"

Sleepy Train,
Lilting, swaying,
Cozy carriage nearly full.
One more space, squeeze in Hippo.
"All aboard, and off we go!"

Sleepy Train climbs
Ever skyward.
Mountain way is steep and high.
Diamond stars,
Try to count them,
Twinkling in the moonlit sky.

Sleepy friends,
Snug and happy,
Nibbling on a bedtime snack.

What's outside?
Take a peep.
Then through the
tunnel, inky black!

Train slows down.
Nearly there.
Snuggle down,
it's time to sleep.
"Land of Nod"
the driver cries,
but everyone has ...

Land of
Nod

... closed their eyes.

Shhh! Shhh! Shhh!

Night-night!

Good
Night!